PROM GIRLS

A North American Rite of Passage

Copyright © 2010 Lesley Fletcher (text and illustrations)

Copyright © 2010 Christian Shanti-Gagnon (In a Café)

This is a work of fiction. Names, character, places and incidents are either products of the author's imagination or have been used with permission.

Published by Inspiration Import. All rights reserved. No part of this book may be used or reproduced in any manner whatsoever without written permission of the author or Inspiration Import except in the case of brief quotations embodied in critical articles and review.

Prom Girls: A Noth American Rite of Passage

ISBN: 978-0-9865332-0-4

www.prom-girls.com

Book Layout: Custom-book-tique

For bulk order prices or any other inquiries, please contact lesfletcher99@hotmail.com.

PROM GIRLS

A North American Rite of Passage

by Lesley Fletcher

TABLE OF CONTENTS

FORWARD

WHEN MY ELDERLY FRIEND offered her wisdom, I listened. She explained to me how she had learned, over the years to "listen"; not just to others and what is around her but listen to herself first and to all elements of life.

When my young daughter offered her wisdom, I listened. She explained that in order to know who you are and where you are in life you need first to acknowledge the history that brought you to this point.

Ultimately, although I listened to advice, I owe this book and all its contents to myself for adopting these offerings while life around me seemed not to.

As I painted the watercolours, their characters spoke to me. As I listened, I found the stories to be filled with youth, nostalgia, innocence, humour, and most of all, truth.

The desire to share these illustrations and their stories propelled me to personal enlightenment, as I drew on experiences I believed were long since forgotten. At the same time, it brought to light my love story with Montreal in all of its glory, distinction, charm, and cultural diversity.

This collection of short stories follows a seventeen-year-old male, who is a composite of my experiences with the males I have encountered over my lifetime. His story picks up just before prom in his last year of high school, as he goes to pick up his tuxedo.

Intertwined within this tale is the story of the traditional prom night "rite of passage" in Montreal, which is clearly distinct in its vast uniqueness while simultaneously remaining steeped in tradition.

Once in a while, I will take you off the beaten path as I share some personal experiences, and as the prom girls and boys visit lesser known but equally real life scenarios. I have invited guest "authors" to help me capture some areas that are unique to only them and at the same time lend some sugar and spice.

This book is a celebration of Montreal's cultural melting pot; its love affair with youth, ethnicity, and struggle—and a journey into what it is like to be seventeen years old in the 21st century. I hope to share a true sense of joy, adventure, and promise as well as cultivate respect and appreciation for the pressures youth face in today's fast moving world. Happy Prom Night, grads.

You have earned the Night. Enjoy!

IN A CAFÉ

Chatters of teenage girls
Next to me, in the smoking section.

They are debating whether,
For their Graduation Ball,
Six months from now,
They should hire a limousine.

Oh to be sixteen again
(....except for the heartbreaks).

And the gods are laughing
Young, old, ageless

by Christian-Shanti Gagnon

THE LIMO

JUST THINKING OF THE word "limo" conjures up visions of wealth, partying, elegance, VIP status, comfort, and a feeling of achievement and excitement—especially when you are seventeen.

It is no wonder that by mid to late January of the graduating year the word "limo" is whispered with reverence and fascination. It's either a conversation maker or breaker, but one thing for sure is that no one should underestimate the power of that seemingly innocuous word Limo.

The Talk Starts Like This:

"We have to book now. My cousin has a limo company and my mom told me he has like so many cars in his fleet (that's what he calls it), and already three are booked! They book up really fast so we need a deposit, then my mom will call my cousin, and he's going to give us a really good deal. Trust me."

The Decision:

They decide that the best way to go is top of the line, straight up, because already they are getting an amazing price. They also decide that, since they are getting a great price (they are paying cash, which will save them 15% extra) they will book the Escalade. It's humongous, has room for twelve, and is by far the best ever. They will hire it to pick them up, stay, and drop them off. It is luxury at its finest.

This decision took three weeks because there was a lot of negotiating as to who would get to take advantage of this fantastic opportunity they got, thanks to the cousin.

The Money:

Everyone manages to convince their parents that this is the best deal out there and all of their friends are going in the limo. They throw in the appropriate hint about safety because their date isn't going to be driving. This is added insurance and a perfectly legitimate way to make sure they nail the deal.

Parents everywhere are so relieved (cue in music to "Leader of the Pack") and pleased with the planning. They are so proud that their little dears did it all on their own. So proud, in fact, that they actually run to the bank machine so their child does not miss this momentous opportunity…and finally stop the endless discussion that has dominated every single waking hour…thanks to the cousin (reprise of "Leader of the Pack").

The Bad News:

The twelve-person Escalade is available because the city's most notorious family cancelled due to some ongoing criminal investigation. Who cares? The kids have the Escalade they so dreamed of. The very proactive cousin has already booked the driver, and everyone knows the best drivers are booked early.

So how can this be bad news?

We live in Quebec, that's why. In Quebec any limo, no exceptions, cannot carry more than eight people, even though it seats twelve. This law is one that even the shadiest of limo companies will not break. They would rather have an ear amputated than break this law. (Conscientious and suspicious parents check this absurdity to find it is, in fact, a law).

The kids don't get it. Everyone knows that for the prom you can break the law, but the cousin won't budge. Something is starting to smell bad, thanks to the cousin.

The prom-going-cousin-of-the-cousin is starting to get very defensive. Probably she, the mother, and the cousin knew this all along, right? Her friends all wonder, "Did they even put down a deposit themselves? Or did they increase everyone else's deposit to pay for the cousin-of-the-cousin?"

It turns out they just call the cousin a "cousin." He's not really a blood relative. They just call him a cousin because when they were kids they called his mother "aunt." So he ended up being a cousin. He's more of a *comparie*, like family, but not quite. His mother and the prom girl's mother were *comare*. Point finale. They're family. Therefore, the title of cousin still stands.

The Dilemma:

Who is getting kicked out of the limo? Four of your closest BFFs, that's who. And so it begins. They cannot find another limo, because they *are* actually booking up pretty quickly. However, everyone is adamant that they must have the now illustrious Escalade.

They know who they would like to kick out, but then they will lose the limo entirely.

The Timing:

It is mid-February and everyone knows what that means…Valentine's Day!

Okay, now we're talkin'.

Everyone knows that it is a fact that Valentine's Day is a make it or break it event for many would-be prom dates. It is a simple matter of sitting back and seeing what comes out in the wash. Everyone has their own strategy to snare the perfect prom date. Please don't call him a date. What do we call him? Companion? Person? Someone? Boyfriend? Let's just call him a friend; someone I like, but that I don't "like" like. Just don't call him a prom date. That's just so lame.

The Great Limo Dilemma should take care of itself by the end of February. The situation only requires four casualties and based on last year's Valentine's Day stats it is very doable.

The Follow up Result to Valentine's Day:

Seven of the twelve Escalade riders are Valentine's Day casualties. There was sure to be a multitude of un-friending happening in the following days.

The deposit money is gone, because the cousin already booked the driver and gave him a "down deposit."

The cousin of the cousin probably won't even go to the prom. Her non-date, non-boyfriend (named "Baller" lol) did not come through quite as expected on Valentine's Day. She decided to go to the prom with someone from another school because:

- One of the girls going to her own prom bought the exact same dress as she did, and her mother won't let her get another one. Mothers really, *really* don't get it and that's a proven fact!
- The Limo is a twenty-two seat Lincoln Navigator! (Driving in from Ottawa equals more $$$.)
- She found herself a Weekend Millionaire! STATUS! Everyone is heading up to Tremblant right after the dinner to her date's place to party all weekend.
- She hates Baller now, ever since Valentine's Day. What kind of a name is Baller anyway?

BTW, the reason for the other five Valentine's Day casualties remains a mystery. There are rumours, but no real facts have surfaced…yet. It is said to be "complicated." Lmao!

The End Result:

After the seven Valentine's Day casualties, the five remaining prom goers are:

- All girls. Going to arrive at the prom in a late 70's model deep purple black limo, which they managed to rent for a pretty decent price;

- Very lucky to have even *found* a limo the month before prom;

- A little put out. The father of one of the girls will be the limo driver. Dad recently landed a weekend freelancing gig. He wants to add a bit of income to his full-time salary as a CEO. But it's only a twenty minute drive, and at least Dad won't be at the dinner. TG;

- Wondering what the heck is wrong with everyone these days—don't they know this is supposed to be happy carefree time in their lives? *Excited!*

THE GRAD COMMITTEE

EACH YEAR THE GRAD committees work tirelessly on behalf of their fellow students to plan a well-constructed and fun-filled prom night. At least one teacher is assigned to each of these committees. The teacher oversees progress and essentially has the last word. Endless questions, ideas, logistics, and drama are all part of the committee. Kudos to the teacher who volunteers for this position…and double kudos to the kids who are a part of it.

There are fund-raisers, yearbook submissions, posters, meetings, votes, arguments, and tons of behind-the-scenes action. They must decide who they can get to set up and administer the prom dress registration? Who will represent and set up Facebook group? Post the pictures? Twitter? Paint the Posters? The list of responsibilities and chores seems infinite and, unsurprisingly, there are those who come to bat, those who drop the ball, and way too many in the spectator section—complete with cheers and boos.

Only thing is, this is not a game. No siree. It is a very vital part of the celebration. Those who have completed their five high school years, despite all of the various factors, dynamics, and dilemmas, have earned it. The pride and spirit of the prom are every bit as real as life gets, and every bit as important.

Although the prom checklist is mind boggling, the prom committee members, united in purpose, will often sacrifice certain essentials of teenage life, all for the sake of a glorious prom night.

The Initial Prom Checklist is but one small element of the entire production:

- Dinner cruise – Old Port – re: Parents: cocktail only, no dinner, no dance

- Hotel Dinner Reception – additional evening invites available how many each??

- Photographer

- DJ

- Band – more fundraising? Book them now?

- Fundraising

- Cost of tickets

- Plan evening theme or event

- King and Queen voting? Pre-selection? Criteria?

- Flowers and Crowns and Flowers

- Speeches of thanks

- Opening father daughter, mother son dance, song selection

- Print tickets

- Invitation restrictions?

- Decorations

- Logistics

- Etc.

- Etc.

- Etc.

Luckily, the committee has access to the notes and checklists from previous years. With this history passed down year after year, it is no wonder that within the school itself lie the roots of the traditional prom.

Although each year the new committee does its best to improve on last year's prom by interjecting its own signature, so to speak, it is no secret that to scrap all tradition and start anew is an impossible scenario. There are far too many details, far too few volunteers, and too little time and support for much change to take place.

The extreme efforts for a great celebration are ultimately engraved in a soft stone to keep it simple. To keep it simple is a grave understatement to those who sweat it out to make it happen!

Very simply, the tradition *will* continue, with slight changes. There is comfort in these traditions. Those who wish to treat themselves to a traditional prom night in Montreal cannot go far wrong.

With special thanks to the teachers, who somehow manage their jobs, their own families, extra activities within the school, administrative duties, and marking—and for the time they spend to help nurture other people's children with their wisdom and guidance. These selfless teachers form relationships of trust and care, only to have to bid their students good-bye (and rightfully "good riddance," to some) year after year.

"Cocktail"

Corsage Exchange

Limo

Reception cocktail

Dinner

Dance

Hotel

Club(s)

Beauty's

Mt. Royal Sunrise

Coffee

Hotel

Lose Virginity

Brunch – next day

(Sleep is an option) Done…

Bring on the Summer!

It is likely to be the longest summer of your entire life from now until retirement.

ENJOY!

THE TUX

I ORIGINALLY HAD DECIDED, when embarking on this project that I would not use any names in order to, perhaps protect the innocent. I'm going back on that decision for this one guy. I tried to resist, but he's just bigger than life and too much for even me to handle. He's the one that won't be ignored.

Allow me to introduce Baller. He is the first son of parents who recently immigrated to Montreal. His real name is "insert-gawd-awful-name-here," hence the self-imposed handle. Now if you grew up back in the day, you might have a whole other connotation tied to his nickname. Please take note that the word "baller" is simply the new vernacular for "cool." It suits Baller to a "T" because there is no doubt he is one cool dude.

We all know the archetype of this guy, either personally or from a far distance, but we do know him. He is the one that won't be denied.

He is the captain of a high school team and a jerk (this is questionable to some). The girls go out of their way to get his attention, and he is where the expression "man crush" originated by what seems to be an entourage. Some guys think he's a total idiot, but he's just so entertaining that he's always surrounded. There is never a dull moment when you hang with Baller. He believes in having his friends' backs, that friendship rules. He will do almost anything to help a 'friend' and not ask for a return on the favour. There is of course the factor of understanding that he does in fact expect the same consideration to come back to him. If the same sort of favour is not returned he keeps a mental note that exceeds all of his other memory capabilities and there will be repercussions that far surpass the norm. Baller is a complicated yet simple guy that keeps all who cross his path intrigued and in awe of his powerful personality. He's raw and vulnerable and impossible to pin down.

Although he is flunking math, he plans to go into something with computers at CEGEP— because he sincerely wants to please his parents (eyelid pulled down by pinkie of left hand). He is hands down the best hacker the school has ever educated. On that note, he is still working on changing that math mark.

Baller is both a badass and is charming as hell. He gets the most tips of all the employees every shift at Tim's. The guys he works with love him for that. He gets amazing marks on most of his assignments, but only because they are written by someone with less to do on the weekend. He loves to party and have a good time. Baller plans to be a millionaire by the time he's thirty, and somehow you believe he will pull it off. There is a host of really solid reasons to stay on this guy's good side or just avoid him completely.

The Conversation:

So Baller asks his parents, "I wanna rent a tux instead of buying a suit for prom. When you rent, it already comes with shoes, a shirt, tie, and a cumbersome. The one I want is on special, and I know you guys are a bit tight for cash, so is it okay?"

What's really going on in Baller's head?

I know you may think the answer to that question is "not much," but you couldn't be further from the truth.

Baller needs money. He has hit on all his "usuals" just to find that he still hadn't paid them back for the last couple of loans. They were being really vicious about a few bucks. Unbelievable.

Further, there is a good chance that he is in love with the hottest babe in the world. She begged him so sweetly to get a tux that goes with her dress. She told him that blue would be the perfect complement to her pink prom gown. He decided to keep all this a secret from his buddies. He didn't want them to be giving him the eye with prom so close. It was just too good.

Luckily, he found the perfect tux. It's not quite blue, but close enough. It's turquoise, and they only had one. Yes, a bit of Baller luck goes a long way! The tux rental guy confirmed it was a one-of-a kind choice, and he knew on the spot that it had to be the tux for him. It was Karman, or whatever. He put down the deposit already.

He has big plans for the tux. He has given it a lot of thought. He hopes his girl appreciates what he's doing for her. First he's switching out the frilly faggot shirt and wearing his new white t-shirt because let's face it, he's buff and a tux with a t-shirt is like the perfect look for him. He's seen this look on TV award shows and in magazines but he is sure none of his contemporaries have the guts he has to actually just do it!

Because of the special colour of the tux, he will finally get a chance to wear the white belt he bought in New York on spring break last year. The buckle itself was worth ten times what he paid for the belt. It's freaking huge!

 The Shoes? Forget it. The ones at the rental place were like cardboard boxes, and not only that—they didn't even have a size fourteen for him! Anyway, his new basketball shoes are comfortable and shiny and make him a good one and a half inches taller. What can he say? Things are looking too good.

Screw the tie. Don't need it with the t-shirt. He decided to keep it in his pocket to give to his girl. She will love him even more! How unique and romantic can you get? It's a bow tie with an elastic, just like those flower things all the girls wear on their wrists, only difference is it won't fall apart – she can keep it forever! LOL. He can hardly wait to see her expression when he puts it on her wrist. Chicks love that stuff and not only that, man! The color is turquoise, which is way nicer than blue. It's in the bag baby— *in the bag.*

There's more. Get this: His baseball cap is practically made to measure to go with the tux. It's covered with turquoise and diamond rhinestones. Seriously, chill. He's a genius. Math? Huh. Who needs it? BTW, what the hell is a cumbersome? Wat? Do they think he's going to rob a bank or something?

He was positive that he and Pink were going to blow-out everyone in their path when they made their entry anywhere. With his great style and her amazing looks, they would def rule the night.

The Result

This guy can charm his own parents. They are more than happy to fork over the money for the tux. They are more proud than even he knows or realizes, as he is the very first one in the family to have the opportunity to graduate from high school and go to college. The math? Who needs advanced math anyway? He is a computer **genius. A genius in the family!** Who would have seen that coming? Baller is going to do so **well in math at CEGEP.** They have cleared a special pathway for kids just like him, kids that the teachers were biased against. Baller said it himself. It happens all the time to immigrant kids. Send that teacher to the old country and see how much he picks on the kids there! He calls himself Baller! Even though he told them, they forget what the word means now. What they do know is it means something very flattering to them as parents. What a kid. What a great kid!

THE CORSAGE

MY FRIEND JEAN ANN was kind enough to share her non-prom story with me. It is nothing new that each year there are graduates who choose not to attend their prom. About one in ten people I have come across did not go to their own prom (including myself – lol). Inevitably, however, there is still a story to tell. Something about being seventeen years old is so very special that it allows us all to hold the memories for a lifetime.

Today the corsage doesn't hold too much meaning. More often than not, it is not a surprise nor is it particularly romantic. It does not serve a purpose other than to follow tradition and perhaps solidify the fact you do indeed *have* an escort. Parents are usually given the task of choosing, picking up, paying for, and sometimes even delivering the flowers to their daughter or son and their respective dates.

It wasn't always that way. The following story demonstrates yet again another angle of prom night.

It's all about the Corsage

"I'm a Mennonite farm girl from a German community in rural Oklahoma. Since I attended a private protestant school, I didn't experience prom back in the late 1960's. Mennonites don't dance. And there could be no king and queen of prom, because that would exalt people and that's not very Mennonite either.

"So, why do I get to tell my story? Because we had a pseudo prom event called "The Sweetheart Banquet" on or about Valentine's Day. Only juniors and seniors received invitations, but students who were older, younger, or from a different school could attend as long as a junior or senior from the Bible academy accompanied them.

"I attended both years, but I don't really remember who I invited. You see, I changed boyfriends more frequently than I changed hairstyles. By the time I reached my senior year of high school, I had dated every eligible boy in the school, plus a few more from nearby schools and communities. Unfortunately, the best-looking boys in the community were my cousins and, hey, I said I was from Oklahoma—not Arkansas!

"You may wonder, 'Why is it all about the corsage?' Well, that's how we measured the value of relationships. Here are some benchmarks:

- Gardenia Corsage: Six months as a couple

- Roses Corsage: Pretty much a year

- Orchid Corsage: Well, the next step had to be a promise ring!

"Now, you might ask, *How can she remember what kind of corsage she got? She changed boyfriends so frequently, and can't even remember who she dated!* Easy. Because I got carnations! Cheap, boring, already made up, no thought to it, easy-to-match-the-boutonnière-and-corsage-to-the-dress carnations! I was always so embarrassed when all I got was a frumpy carnation corsage that said, 'This may be our only date, so she's not getting an expensive flower!' Ah. The high price of window-shopping!"

KA-CHING!

SOMEWHERE ALONG THE LINE, prom got out of hand in the acquisition department. This can be attributed (but not solely) to the basic fact that every generation wants to provide a better life for their children than what they themselves had. This aspect of human nature prevails in our times, at least here in Montreal and most of North America where the population has recently enjoyed, for the most part, a prosperous time. The over-consumption and accumulating of extras is an almost universal theme to make it seem they have—you got it—mega bucks. Nothing is out of the reach with Visa, lines of credit, cash income, and a parent's pure, unadulterated love for the grad.

Now for the shopping list…

The only optional items on this list are the "little bags."

The checklist is enormous and everything is essential to those who have been brought up with the perpetual "silver spoon." The silver spoon population has grown and changed remarkably over generations. At one time, it included only royalty, the very wealthy, doctors, lawyers, and the lucky. In the 21st century this category has expanded to include the millionaire next door, the former DINKS, the everyday Joe, the Me Generation, who have the need to prove it's *just not true*, and the immigrants who believe that with opportunity comes the requirement to display their accomplishments. What better way is there to demonstrate that than through their children?

So here is the standard list for those fortunate enough to have it fulfilled. The cost is astronomical, and the list applies almost solely to the prom girls. The guys seem to be okay with the very basic needs: A rented tux, jeans, socks boxers, and a shirt; and a haircut, gel, and cologne. A commentary on sexual differences will not follow. Some things just don't change and for some reason, most can and do find comfort in that.

Grad dress: To be worn underneath the gown, preferably light in color, and nothing you will likely see your grad in again unless there is a baptism in the very near future.

Purse to go with Grad Dress: Small, plain, and just big enough for cell phone, camera, and lip-gloss.

Shoes to go with Grad Dress: These are easy, hands down. The lingerie is a challenge, and the rest could break the budget wide open.

Little black dress: To wear after the prom.

Small purse to go with the little black dress worn after the prom: Self-explanatory, as long as it has some sort of kick to it.

The Prom Dress: This dress is a crucial part of the evening, although it will be worn for approximately only six hours. No expense is spared for the prom dress. What is essential to the success of the entire event is the dress's quality, style, colour, and originality. The dress must be flattering on the wearer, and individuality is top priority. Mothers are particularly intuitive to this necessity. Price is no object if the attendee finds the perfect dress.

The tradition of the stores on St. Hubert Street cannot be understated. For generations the merchants there have provided a tremendous variety at a substantially lower price than other locations.

As a part of that prom tradition, the attendee (accompanied not by her clique of friends, but more usually by her mother), first investigates *the Street*. Here they are privy to thousands of prom dresses in thousands of colors and styles. It doesn't take long to become disoriented, as the thousands of choices begin to all look like the same dress. Nonetheless, tradition and ritual require the attendee to bravely troop down to the Street and as part of the list of "things to do,"

spend hours searching for the perfect dress, only to return home exhausted, disenchanted, and often dress-less.

Luckily, Mom can easily find a dress for the night out in the same stores, as it serves a dual purpose of mother-daughter time and cuts back a tiny bit on the actual hours logged for prom purchases. A happy mother goes a long, long way when it comes to prom shopping.

The very most flabbergasting mystery here is that in spite of the similarities of the dress selection in every store on this street, it is in fact a very rare occurrence to tag a fellow prom goer wearing an exact duplicate of your dress.

The secret to this mystery must be revealed at this point. In spite of the mass exodus to St. Hubert Street, a good majority of prom girls buy their dress on the "sly." The number of trips to New York, Paris, Florida (yes, I said Florida) and umpteen other long distance destinations demonstrates the fact that the prom dress is a virtual *phenomenon.*

The silk, the organza, the wedding white, the patterns, shapes, colours, fit, length... Endless selection and endless hunting and seemingly endless confusion until the right one is found. And then it is *done*.

And…time, naturally, to immediately post your style, colour, and general description on the prom dress registry belonging to your school, just to be certain that no one else will be wearing "your dress" that evening.

The bag to go with the prom dress must be equally fitting for the occasion. It must be unique and only big enough to hold the essentials. Most importantly, it absolutely must have some pizzazz!

Next, we must find the "after after-prom" attire. Each Prom goer already has these clothing items in her wardrobe—but this is the prom! That calls for something new.

Jeans: Very important. Top: Of utmost importance. No expense is spared for this casual ensemble.

A big bag is important here. This is unlike anything found in the current wardrobe. This is the perfect chance to acquire a new bag that will get through the whole summer, with the promise to keep it forever (well, at least into university…wink).

If the prom goer is doing the hotel thing, or even just staying at a friend's house, then it is crucial to have the requisite pajama pants or boxers with tank (built-in bra optional). Equally important is a sweatshirt for the more modest in order to run around the hotel from room to room or outside if necessary; or even to serve as warmth for the "bed on the floor," or as a pillow in less-than-adequate accommodations.

One extra-large tote to carry all the peripherals and stuff the "used" clothing in.

Add to this the miscellaneous essentials: A new makeup case (complete with new make-up), bottle of touch up nail polish, mini hairspray, shampoo, tooth brush and toothpaste, conditioner, new deodorant (yes), an alternate outfit—just in case—other miscellaneous random "essentials," and you are almost done!

Almost done?

Hair cut prior to prom night

Hair color changes, changes back, extensions (optional)

Hair done on prom day

Make up bought for prom

Make up application prom day

Acrylic nails

Nail polish

Manicure

Pedicure

Massage——Stresssssss

Waxing

The shopping part is almost complete! Only shoes and undergarments remain.

Please note: The price of limo, flowers, prom dinner tickets, spending money, hotel stay, brunch, alternate activities, drinks, admissions, and extra snacks are not yet included in the budget.

Cash registers ring, credit cards are hot to the touch with excessive use, banks accounts are over drawn, lines of credit kick in, patience is dwindling and prom is still about five months away.

KA-CHING KA-CHING KA-CHING!

THIRTEEN CHOICES - *THE STING*

PROM GIRLS, LISTEN UP. I have a plan, but it is crucial that it be kept a secret. Mum's the word, if you know what I mean. Follow it to the letter and you won't be sorry. Would I steer you wrong?

First, you must decide exactly what kind of under garments you will require for all of your functions and needs. I just took you clothes shopping, so to be successful in acquiring the lingerie on your wish list in the underwear department, please refer back to the basics of the "Prom Wardrobe Essential Requirements." This, of course, will require a serious amount of time consuming pre-shopping. However, if you follow the plan, I feel confident enough to guarantee a minimum 50% success rate in acquiring the perfect prom under-attire.

Now that I have your attention here are the **instructions**: Whenever (stress "whenever") you are shopping, or even go out with your parents in **public**, you must (stress on the word "must") wear your oldest underwear, or at the very least **underwear** that you know they hate. This is called "setting the ground work." A savvy few of you have already applied this technique in other areas. You can advise your fellow enthusiasts of the need for focus, patience, and of course a tiny bit of acting thrown in for good measure.

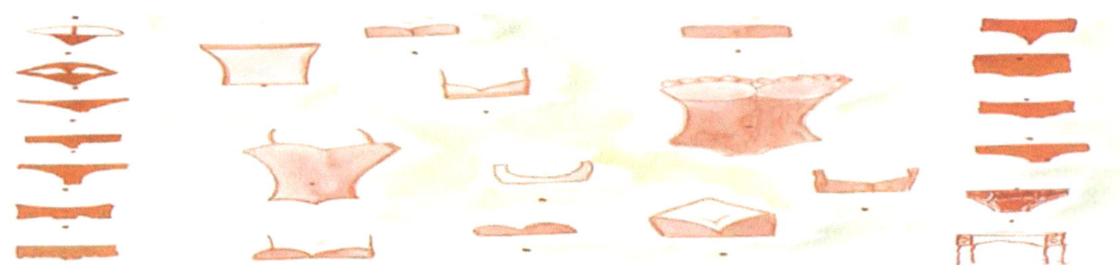

Then, whenever you are at the receiving end of either remarks or "looks," you simply roll your eyes (practice not necessary – everyone can do it) in disgust. If you are not the eye-rolling type, then look embarrassed, ashamed, or whatever works best for *you*. Before you know it, your dad will be whispering to your mom, and she will be off on a secret underwear mission of her own to take care of the "problem" discreetly.

Hint: This works especially well if you wear a white bra that has been "accidentally" thrown in with the dark load a few times. Together, with sporting a too-tight string thong while modeling a pale, tight, slinky Prom dress, it's almost *too* good. You may want to save it as a last measure.

Remember: You know what you really want. Actually, "need" is a better word. Again, I can't stress the importance of patience in this undertaking.

Next step: Take your Mom to the largest, most confusing, busiest lingerie store. Don't forget to let her know that "everyone" was buzzing about the amazing sale going on. This is Montreal. I don't expect this part to offer any difficulties whatsoever. Do not try this in Plattsburgh.

Places everyone! ACTION! You're on! Spend as much time as humanly possible "deciding" and soliciting "advice" from your very kind mother. Be nice. Even try on a few things she suggests, and then dejectedly reject them. Do not deviate from the plan. When you find the exact item you want, and you ask and she says no (as she undoubtedly will), you must persevere.

Have your mom search through hundreds of bikinis for the color and size you want, and then change your mind about everything and start again. It would be beneficial to your cause to pretend to be searching with her. Get the sales girls involved as this just makes it more real. Creating chaos in a chaotic environment is not that difficult. Do this as many times as can, until your own nerves can't take it anymore.

Agree to go home when she gets fed up. And she will. Hint Number Two: It is advisable to have a healthy, hearty breakfast, and to wear comfortable shoes in order to outlast her, but I feel confident that you can do so unaided! You may add a few tears at your (imagined) weight gain or misshapen body if necessary.

That night, following some sulking around, convince mom that because she loves you, you will continue the great undergarment hunt. Then change your mind. Then change it back. Then, have your friend call to invite you to go with her to the same store but in another location (very important detail). Make sure your mother hears snippets of the conversation. Carefully explain that your friend said there was different stock at the other store, and you would probably have found something but for the fact that mom was too tired the first time around. Try to look both hopeful and pathetic. The preceding instructions should be re-read as needed. There is no room for error!

Then sit back prom girl. Payola time. Politely take the money, or credit or debit card you are offered (don't act too surprised or go overboard on the thanking, or you may blow it), and go buy what you had decided on months ago.

And remember, *please*, to keep all this hush-hush. After all, isn't it still a bit personal to be talking about underwear in the first place? Shhhh!

WARNING: While this method may be used to fulfill a number of similar needs, it is not advised to overuse this strategy. Overuse will fail to produce the desired results.

SHOES (AND ANKLES)

MONTREAL IS SECOND ONLY TO Rome in the shoe department, in my opinion, but substantially much less expensive. So I'm going to bump it to first place based on cruel economic times. It is virtually a shoe shoppers' Mecca. NYC is not even in the running; however, rumour has it that Burlington, Vermont is a great place to buy boots.

My point is that finding shoes is a breeze in Montreal, and the prom girls have no problem acquiring several pairs that suit all the shoe requirements for the afternoon, evening, overnight, and brunch attire.

I won't venture into the actual shopping days that are swallowed up to meet the requirements of prom. Rather, I will share a personal memory to pay homage to my own mother, who was just so cute as she related her "I was a teenager once, too" story to me many years ago.

Her home town of Leslie (I know, I know. But she denied it), Scotland was decidedly not a shoe haven. In fact, it remains doubtful to me if they even *had* a shoe store there in 1939. My mother, by the way, was a self-confessed shoe addict all her life. Although she didn't go overboard buying shoes, her collections remained extensive because she kept them perfect and forever. She was in love with every pair.

Similar to other teenage girls over the generations, my mum was a mischievous little dare devil. Of course, this statement is made relative to the time in history that she grew up in.

She spoke of an annual ankle competition that took place in the neighbouring town and the fact that her best friend since kindergarten had begged her to join her in entering it. My mum tried as she might to get permission from my grandmother, but to no avail. At each attempt, she was quickly dismissed with, "Don't be daft." The loose translation goes something like this: "If you dare enter that foolishness, there will be hell to pay."

Not one to be held back from enjoying life at seventeen, my mother and her BFF came up

with a plan. They found a way to make a vegetable dye to tint their legs, coal to make the stocking line straight up the back and acquired two pairs of high heels while they pounded out a palatable plan to spend that day together away from my gran's watchful eyes.

It was not uncommon to be gone the entire day, given that most destinations were reached by foot. They entered the contest, paid their fee, and lied about their age (the requirement was 19 years old, but there was no ID back then). Then they patiently and excitedly awaited instructions.

They were assigned numbers, and then when their number was called they strolled across a curtain at the theatre that fell to about sixteen up from the stage floor. It was a completely anonymous showing, with the judges unable to view anything but the mid calf of the leg and of course the glorious competing ankles.

Well, my mother won that popular contest (she giggled and blushed as she related this part of the tale to me), and consequently her name, along with the winning ankle photo, was announced in the village newspaper. This newspaper was distributed to the surrounding boroughs. She hadn't thought of that fact. Never even gave it a thought, She was too enthralled with having bragging rights over something so naughty.

Although her best friend told her that her name was in print, my mother never got to see it, nor did her parents. The day of delivery of that day's edition my gran "accidentally" crumpled it into the fire she was starting in my mum's bedroom, while my aggravated grandfather spouted loudly about missing his nightly read.

I would like to thank my grandmother for saving my mum from the wrath of Granddad that evening by doing only what a mother can do for her child. Thanks, too, to my mum for sharing with me her story of the timelessness of youth: Her story that took place on the backdrop of the brink of World War II. I miss you, Mum. Forever.

VALEDICTORIAN

Traditional:

"AND SO FELLOW STUDENTS, as we move on together in solidarity toward our separate futures, remember to follow your dreams. You can do it! We all can!"

Polite applause: Proud smiles of the principal, teachers and parents; hoots and hollers of the popular vote grads; and subtle eye rolls, nudges, whispers, and shifting flood the auditorium.

Not So Traditional:

"And so, guys, if it turns out you can't follow ur dreams cus life's a bitch and just gettin' in the way, it's still cool. If you have to chill cus u can't do it anymore, it's ok. Promise urself though to hang onto those dreams anyway cus life will still be there when you're ready.

And you know that song "Waiting for the World to Change"? Ditch that bs from ur head. Why wait for someone else to change the world for you? You got ideas – you got a brain – use it and make the frikken world change the way YOU want it to. The guy who wrote that song got it all wrong.

"Be a part of the change.

"I barely made it through high school but I have a voice and I know how to use it. I got technology down. I'm headin' vocational cus that's what I wanna do… so I have what it takes to hang onto my dreams – for now."

THE "COCKTAILS-BY-THE-POOL" PARTY

AS A PART OF EXPLORING the traditional prom, I introduce the pre-prom "cocktail" party where, in some cases, parents of the attendees may join *if* they are invited. Punch and hors d'oeuvres are the norm, while everyone gets a chance to mingle with those they haven't met or giggle with those they know well. Generally, there are about eight prom goers and their dates, and likely more if there is lots of space or the hosting prom girl is very popular.

If it's a nice day, the guests are commonly herded out to the back yard deck. If the host has a pool, it is inevitable that the photos will be around the pool. Did I mention tradition?

Invited parents are decidedly like fish out of water at this function, as they haven't really had the chance to meet other parents over the course of the five years of high school, save a few events here and there. But attend they do, as they really don't want to miss an opportunity to see their prom girls in a grown up setting, and catch a glimpse of the dresses (not to mention the dates). Prom night is just full of nostalgia. It comes to the parents' minds that they used to know all of their kids friends' parents, and acted as the main intermediary in setting up and supervising play dates in what seems like just yesterday.

With the astronomical advent of social networking sites, little card invitations are not necessary anymore as the invites are more easily managed online. For instance, if one person responds "no" or "maybe," then the hostess has the ability to immediately replace that person with another of her friends to ensure a good showing at her party. When they respond "yes," the response registers online. This provides a beginning basis for others who might consider attending. It is my contention that it is important for the inviter to get some "yeses" right away, or the party risks failure before it is even in progress.

The networking sites online are also a great forum to post the thousands of photos taken of prom night. They are posted to these sites virtually "live," because they can and are being directly sent to their page via their phone or PDA just as they are happening.

On the other hand, parents have, for the most part, a little trouble keeping up with the latest technology. It just goes excessively fast. Being brought up in the digital era is undoubtedly a big advantage. You are just used to thinking digital, and nothing is a big surprise. The pace technology has been moving at is one which the kids of these times have adapted to readily.

All in all, the cocktail party is representative of what the future may hold for its attendees. Idle chitchat, well behaved and well dressed, a few little flaws to gossip about, a tiff that takes place for all to pretend they don't notice, and a mixture of both socially shy and boisterous people. Not to mention food, drink, and organization. Hmmmmmm. Sounds a little like real life, doesn't it?

Suspiciously MIA in the "round the pool shot" is Baller, who later fessed up to spiking the punch while downing most of the hors d'oeuvres delightfully laid out and totally irresistible to feed his constant hunger.

Also missing is the rest of the gang, as technology has not caught on with some of the older generation who insist on "preserving film" while using a digital camera. Further missing is the concept that they have the ability to view the shot they just took.

Into the THE RECEPTION

WHILE THERE ARE MANY venues to choose from, tradition calls for the school's Prom Committee to follow previous years' protocol. As a result, it ends up for the most part at a large reception room, where dinner is served or buffet set out. A DJ is hired, and extra tickets are offered for attending family to join (at least until the father/daughter, mother/son dance). It is an unwritten rule that adults stick with adults and dare not glance at the surrounding tables. It is further understood that *if* your prom goer needs something, they will, in fact, be able to find you. This, in my opinion, is the beginning of payback for the years of "satellite tables" the kids endured during holiday get-togethers.

It is supposed to be a tender occasion where memories, once ignited, are recalled and precious last moments are enjoyed. The reality looks to run a different gambit as the table hopping, mischief, and energy takes over the atmosphere. Once relaxation sets in, the adult setting changes dramatically due to the youth that rules the night. And that is the way it is supposed to be.

THE DINNER

(AKA "BALLER'S GRAND ENTRANCE")

AS SOON AS HE ENTERED the room, he could feel the atmosphere, feel the looks directed his way, and sense the heightened excitement in the air.

Baller was truly in his element. The only, only thing he wasn't crazy about was that he wasn't going to be sitting with his boys. As he took his place beside Pink, he ensured that he had a direct visual of their table. He really didn't care if Pink noticed his strategic seating or not. It was his night too. He was already tiring of the attention she needed. What about him?

Pink was starting to look annoyed (again). What was it with these chicks? All he was doing was texting and calling his very best friends. How insecure was she? He still couldn't figure out why she didn't gush at his tux. He imagined she was probably blown away and too shy to compliment him. He managed to achieve the expected reaction from the entire table (geeks included) when he removed his Jacket and sat down. Oh yeah, Baller was in da house! It so paid off to go to the tattoo convention they were artists extraordinaire! His six-pack rounded off the look he had spent hours contemplating.

Venus

Pink took one look at Baller's Tux and almost died! She had been so specific with him about it! She deliberately talked and repeated for twenty-five minutes straight about the exact colour of blue she wanted him to wear. What in god's name was so complicated about Midnight Blue? Very dark, almost black but not quite. Not navy blue—no way—too military/prep school. Not bright. Too whatever. Not powder blue even if the seventies were "in." Mediterranean blue. Beautiful but not for a tux. Just a very simple and elegant midnight blue! She even emphasized how it would bring out the color of his dark blue eyes. How many more times could she have explained? OMG! All he heard after all her explaining was "blue"? And even then, the colour

he got so wrong, wrong, wrong. Oh, so very wrong! **Grrrr. Sheesh!**

He did look amazing, though, once he removed the jacket and sat that tight-panted ass down

on the chair. Once he got tired of the hideous cap (ruined his vision to his buds' table), things

were getting *a lot* better. His tattoo was still fresh. Every eye was on him, and Pink had him

(almost) to herself. Reminder (note to self): Always go with him when he buys clothes from

now until the altar. Lol? Altar? Whatever possessed her to utter that word (even if it was in her

own mind)?

Reality quickly took over as she glanced at her wrist with that tacky "surprise!" corsage.

Baller had made such a fuss about it! She had *no* idea at this point how she could possibly lose

the thing! All she knew is that she would, and that ridiculous cap would join it. She was giving

the whole idea some very serious thought when she was brought back to the table with the

distinct sound of ruckus coming from the back of the reception hall. It was none other than

those hopeless friends of Baller.

Before she could figure out what was up, Baller bolted out of his chair. He gave her a sort of

weird look. It was definitely directed at her because he stopped dead and turned to her for a

moment, managing to catch her eye.

Mars

Baller couldn't take his stuffy, boring table even one moment more! Not with his friends

laughing and messing around and stuff. This was ridiculous! He wasn't going to sit at this dead

table that smelled like an Axe commercial and had enough gel to fill a cereal bowl. He made up

his mind to leap to his feet, as dramatically as possible, and show these other guys how to *wake up*. Next thing he knew he was heading for the action, where his friends had already started to hoot and holler, anticipating his arrival. He remembered, as he was heading across the floor, to turn to Pink and throw out his extra-stupendous, sexy, smoldering look. Practicing in the mirror was totally key here. He saw her look of sheer acknowledgement and felt the wave of confidence wash over him as he slowed his stride and cooled his gait and greeted his audience.

Once Baller settled down, feeling completely satisfied that he and the guys had managed to pull off the prank on their math teacher. He'd taken care of the payola with the DJ—a nice joint —to play the two songs he secretly planned to dedicate to Pink. Then he would be prepared to devote the rest of his time and attention to her for the remainder of the night.

The kids were all taken by storm and fits of hilarity when the DJ, true to his "bribe," announced the first dedication of the night: A special dedication from Baller (dude) to his lady (Pink). The DJ was having a blast.

In the same cosmic joke kind of way that seems to stick to Baller like glue, his request gathered a backlash and a stir simultaneously. The DJ, who was totally buzzing at this point, made sure that for his newest best friend, Baller, he caught the attention of the room in a grandiose announcement kind of broadcast. All ears in the place were his as he built up the dedication with expert ease. He then played what he truly believed to be the right dedication song…Lil Wayne's Lollipop Remix, continuing the dedication from Baller to Pink on this very special night.

Teachers were not surprised at all at what they considered was typical Baller antics. The parents in the room were way less than impressed as a decided hush fell over half the room. Baller's popularity, however, sky rocketed. Luckily, Pink understood and believed him right away that there was some sort of mix up. She had been teasing him at school, serenading him with the original Lollipop song, "My Boy Lollipop," and they had even downloaded and sung it together.

Thankfully, Pink (blushing) was laughing just as hard as her classmates. For once Baller was enjoying her directly, rather than basking in the attention that surrounded him in one of his many "fifteen minutes of fame" life was to offer him. She had never looked more beautiful to him.

With rarely a dull moment, Baller served up the proof of his existence over and over again. Circumstances and events surfaced as if by his own design, but no one knew the truth and no one ever would.

THE WALTZ

AS THE STRAINS OF the now familiar track of the "Graduation Song" fill the room, the girls get up together and sway together, while taking in the words and letting those words sink into their ever-changing thoughts and minds:

Hoping for a new beginning
To take me away from my surroundings
So I can finally say goodbye……

Some of them have been together since kindergarten, and will likely attend the same college, many of them in the same program. Then they will go on together, to McGill or Concordia, and still keep in touch. Their numbers, however, will dwindle sooner than they ever thought possible on this night. Some shed tears, some shyly hide them, and yet others wonder why they got up to begin with. Without doubt, notice is taken, feelings aroused and more than a few glances at the future are imagined.

Memories invoked by this song have kept it a new favourite and will remain… Tradition once again takes its hold on the night.

GROUP SHOTS and Dance

WITH THE ADVENT OF the lightening speed of digital upload to the Internet, more and

more common are the group shots. Not to be in a group shot during prom night has almost become social suicide. Given the technology, the rush to the camera has become a cultural must do, and is anticipated to soon become a part of tradition.

Ditto for group dances, wild abandons, camera kisses, promiscuous poses, naughty and suggestive grinding, and same-sex flirtation, all totally without regard for the future that awaits. The pouty, seductive, pursed-lipped poses are common sights now and even commonly acceptable at least peer-to-peer. It has become so common and accepted that even though future employers *do* in fact check out applicants' online profiles, the sheer numbers may indeed formulate acceptance. This is the badge this generation will carry. It aligns itself with generations of taboos. From each era: The Roaring 20's, Prohibition, Rock and Roll, Hippies, Androgyny, and Punks. Youth will find something to differentiate themselves from their parents. Music is a given, but behaviour and mindset is key to the stamp of the current generation, no matter what year it is.

THE CIRCLE DANCE

AS THE CIRCLE DANCE dictates, the teachers hit the floor while their former students surround them and laugh at them and make fool of themselves (again). The teachers laugh along, knowing full well what their ex-charges are thinking—and really don't care. They are celebrating too! The year is done. They have done their best, and they can only hope it serves their students well.

Yes the teachers are having fun, and yes, Mr. Head of the Math Department did "get a room" with Ms. Faculty, just as whispered all year. The late arrivals after third period and prolonged conversations as they engaged in "shop-talk" outside the class room, while they let the students shoot their spitballs and text their friends, was not due to over active hormonal imagination after all.

They were full of hope and abandon, while feeling relief that they would no longer have to hide their relationship.

UP TO THE CONDO CHALET
AT MT. TREMBLANT

THE GIRLS HURRIED AWAY from the reception without even taking time to change as the limo waited outside the hotel lobby for them. From there it is up to Mt.Tremblant for the weekend. Once there, they will meet with other weekend millionaires and get blasted from here to eternity on liberal supplies of coke and pot and booze. Some will just squander their time and lull about while others enjoy some serious partying along with the usual town activities and checking out the tourists.

As an introduction to this story, I would like to explain its origins. Prateek (the contributor) and I became fast friends quite accidentally through Facebook. We both forget the exact circumstances now and laugh. I asked to write as he speaks with his friends, just as they talk on MSN as everyone in his approximate age group have the capability to speak, read, and write. It has to be noted at this point that he is perfectly capable of communicating and writing in the traditional way, too. Below is what I received by email. Totally unexpected and equally totally charming.

SMOKE WAS HIGH IN D AIR

SMOKE WAS HIGH IN D AIR… D clock struck n doodle made a very irritating noise which brought me out of d trance n i stopped thinking about the prom night wich me, roy n vik had decided to skip!! Had a dizzziness in ma head probably due to d excess booze i had (1 full jar…lol), but it seemed it was child's play for roy n vik who even aftr 3 jars didnt show a single sign of shaking,stopping or gettin a feeling of hangover…

We were probably the only 3 guys or probably the only 3 losers who were without dates on our prom night, no girl to dance wid, no girl to hang out wid, no girl to kiss n drop off at d end of d night !!!! I was beginning to wonder are we seriously dat big losers or is it d high standards we have set which is often hard for d girls to match up wid…!!!!!! i dont know abt d other 2, but i really did n do believe i belonged to d latter one.

We had nuthn really to talk abt… Our facial expressions said everythn… missing prom night, cruising all night without any date, ending up in a bar, surrounded by booze n smoke, even a layman would think dat we r bloody junkies… Neways we didnt give a shit!! Soon roy ordered another round of beer on which i said no… We wer havin an argument abt dat n suddenly a cool breeze struck my ear, or i guess our ears….

All d 3 heads turned towards d entrance simultaneously. Saw a sight wich was rare n unforgettable... Literally Saw an angel entering, as if just descended frm heaven sent by GOD jst for me, accompanied by her frnd who was...hmmm…well whom i dont really remember....

Dey both sat on d table just opposite to us. I was dying to talk to her n know her but before i cud get my act together, seeing dem alone, roy n vik waved at dem n went towards them for the introduction.......i quietly followed dem. The girls wer very co-ordial to us, allowed us to sit down wid dem jst to hv a casual conversation ! I honestly wasnt able to believe my luck :)..... i was sitting right next to my dream girl !!!!!!!!!!!!!!!!!

We introduced each other... Yasmine is what that angel's name is!! My other 2 frnds showing deir smartness or desperateness or over smartness or u can call it nethn, dey continued talking wid dem.... Dey wer acting as if only 4 ppl wer sittin on d table n wer trying deir best to impress dose girls...!!! I on d other hand didnt speak much , was keeping to myself, probably cuz i was still thinkin it wasnt real n probably cuz i knew dis girl is way out of my league so even thinking abt her would be stupidity!

Suddenly she looked at me...eye to eye contact.... cant forget that.. as if she wnted to say sumthn really sweet to me.... i was waiting for d words to pour out of her mouth jst like honey........... n she said hey prateek...... can u get me a beer, a bit quickly ??!!i cudnt really reply, jst noded my head n went to get her a beer....

On my way to gettin dat beer i was happy dat she talked... but also another thought kept perstering me dat y did she chose me to get her a drink over d other 2?! probably she saw others wer too busy, n i being d only useless person on dat table, was selected for d task.... It wasnt dat i wasnt willing to fullfil her request, it was jst dat at dat moment i felt like a bloody assistant....... neways i tried forgettin all dat but while returning to d table i saw vik touching yasmine's hand........... my heart came out of my mouth, i went n kept d beer on d table, said "wen u ppl r done.. i'd be waiting outside...." n i stormed my way out........

Outside sitting on d bench alone as i was staring at d stars, taking myself as d biggest loser n d biggest pessimist in d world, cursing my luck n thinking how unjust this world is... i saw sumthn more beautiful dan d stars n d moon sitting jst next to me n looking directly into my eyes.......... yup it was yasmine sittin jst next to me. we exchanged wrds... den she said sumthn wich i cannot forget.. she said "if u want to get sumthn really badly... dont wait for it instead just go for it..."

After tellin dis as she turned n was walkin away..i dont know wht happened, i grabbed her hand, pulled her towards me n i kissed her........ those were d most tender lips i had ever felt..

Aftr d kiss, she said nuthn... All dat happened was a car came by, wid a couple of guys in it shouting out her name so as to get her n her frnd in d car.... She said bye, dropped a paper napkin n went away, didnt even stop.....

I was in a shock, didnt kno how to react..... I kiss my dream girl in a night wen i was drunk, totally pissed off wid my life, myself n my frnds... goin thru d worst night ever wich suddenly transforms into d best night of my life simply by one kiss...... n den seeing her vanishing away in seconds brought my world down. Disgusted i picked up d cloth, it had her phone number ! Wat. lol. I found mself actually laughing out loud.

I never actually had d confidence of chasing out girls but dis one was sumethn different.. sumthn special. Dis so very special paper napkin will be wid me always as it makes a direct contact to an angel...... N trust me dis time i wont screw up n would call her as soon as m ready !

For d first time in life m flowing wid confidence, m willing to do nything to get dat girl but till d time i call her, i'l let d feelin of dat kiss stay along wid me n act as my driving force……..

PRATEEK VARMA, 21 YEARS

Prateek is a Graduate of the National Institute of Technology (NIT) College where he studied Engineering. He is currently working on furthering his education by studying for his MBA in either the USA or Canada. At this time, he calls Vadodara, India, his home base.

His immediate family includes a younger brother, his parents, and grandmother. He hopes to contribute to an improved lifestyle for all of them.

He has always pictured himself apart from the pack, with a strong will and desire to separate himself and take on new and bold challenges. He even has the brave ambition of flying supersonic speed aircrafts (Top Gun style) and be a Marine pilot.

We have developed a strong, mutually respectful, and relaxed friendship that has surpassed my expectations. He is charming, intelligent, ambitious, and laden with what I will call the "It" factor. I have no doubt that Prat will even exceed his own expectations.

ALL THAT GLITTERS

IN SPITE OF THE STUNNING statistics that Montreal boasts, it a metropolis and is still a place where danger lurks. Regardless, it is a city with a vibrancy that attracts all types, and therefore a place where one should be able to relax while continuing to be very aware of the dangers that a city, even one as rare as Montreal, can hold.

There is, as in every city, the Good (which is great), the Bad (which is not), and the Ugly (which is often overlooked).

The next few blurbs are but a glance of the precarious experiences that can, but not necessarily, meet the prom girls on their special night. There are narrow escapes, angels floating around, and disasters in the wings that accompany the tradition. These experiences can become irreversible parts of a fun filled night. They can happen as spontaneously as the fun itself.

The girls have enjoyed a majestic night of pure unadulterated fun and excitement. All were a bit tipsy, but one perhaps more than the others. They continue to have each other's backs, which came in handy during the evening when one noticed a slip into her friend's drink. Yes, these girls have managed to get through the night *UN*-scathed except for the onset of nausea and an eminent hangover.

Another girl, a classmate in fact, had way too much to drink and ended up split from her friends. She was not as lucky. She had been gang raped, and now wandered her way from St. Marc toward Crescent, in hopes of finding a familiar face to help her out. She will not tell her parents or the police right away. Her shame, disorientation, partial memory loss and shock prevented justice from ever having the chance to prevail. This experience will stay with her a lifetime, replacing the vibrant memories that rightfully should have belonged to her and her night.

SLIPPERY SLOPES dans la rue

EVEN THE BEST LAID plans don't always pan out, or may not pan out quite the way they were expected to.

My prom girl here, holding hands, is strolling the night away accompanied by a not-so-likely prom escort, along with her best friend.

Her year started out with the thrill of finally finishing high school like the rest of her fellow graduates. She planned and whispered and texted her way through the final term with a heightened sense of excitement for prom night. As all conscientious daughters, do she kept her mom in the loop all the way and shared her enthusiasm with everyone. It was just an amazing time in her life.

Meeting some random guy outside some building where the social justice committee she was on was donating a cheque, turned out to be life changing for her. No one saw it coming. Not even her. They first met when she found him sitting outside a downtown youth shelter along with his German Shepherd. Being a huge dog lover, she shooed away the other two committee members inside with a promise to be back in just a minute. As she patted and cuddled the dog, his owner began to speak, and in doing, shared his story. The tug on her heart was immediate and she found herself making a promise to see him again no matter what. As fate would have it, he was equally struck with her.

All year she had been caught up with committees, prom, studying, family, friends, sports, volunteering, and extra curriculars, while she held down a part time job. It was no wonder she had no time to meet Mr. Right. It was time for her to experience that part of life for a while, and in her eyes, she had met the perfect candidate to fill that role. Her blinders were firmly set, and her purpose was clear in her mind.

Daring not to tell anyone but her best friend, she set out to develop a foolproof plan to be with him on prom night. There could be no better way to spend her night and no better person with whom to spend it. He was truly the sweetest guy she had met in forever. She squirreled away money as it came her way, opting for bargain basement buys to help finance the two of them on prom night, while accumulating a base for her ultimate plan. Her parents would just have to understand and deal with it. She knew the impact her decision would have.

That's just how it happened. In spite of all the fabulous activity swirling around her, this prom girl ended up quite a few steps away from tradition, and several steps into what was to be her adult life.

The solidification of that night's plans would rock her world forever. It was the manufacturing of a future together with a homeless graffiti artist. She would continue in school to be a social worker. One day her best friend would be her maid of honour. He would take the job the city offered him to beautify the graffiti that marred the city walls. He would stay close with the organization that he had come to depend on, and they would adopt lots of kids that were growing up as he had. They would move in together the following week and live happily ever after.

Life onward from here was not without its struggles—by far—but they did it. They followed through with the plan, moved in together without a care in the world but their love for each other at that moment.

STREET BRAWL ABANDON

EARLIER THIS EVENING, as the girls checked out St. Laurent and St. Catharine, these three managed to get themselves in the middle of a brawl. They all came out okay, thanks to the foot patrol in the area. Who knew it was such a big deal to try to talk down a raging guy? They were only trying to help. When the officer told them that no one should have touched the guy's sleeve when he was in full rage, they were shocked.

They truly wanted to help. Two homeless guys had planted themselves on a piece of dirt on a profitable part of the street when two other guys approached and wanted them off "their" turf. One guy was going ballistic as though the other two were sitting on the crown jewels. The two on the ground knew better than to respond or look at the guy who was in a rage. The girls didn't.

They came through, as previously mentioned, due to foot patrol, and managed to find a way to dance the night away with even more fervor than anticipated. Lesson learned. Maybe.

STARS FOR THE NIGHT

THE "STARS FOR THE NIGHT" were far too busy having fun to notice that one of them was missing. They expected her and her boyfriend to show up anytime. She was reliable and in love. They decided that she was late because she and her boyfriend were making out somewhere. Life was like that, so they never bothered to check their phones. Karaoke ruled the night. "I will Survive" blared through the club for the third time tonight and they were performing like headliners.

The car hit the soft shoulder on a curve at 120 kilometers per hour. Mud-drenched in his white tux and holding his hand out to his beautiful girlfriend wearing her sister's wedding dress, he managed to pull her to safety before the engine caught on fire. They watched together as their evening and possessions went up in smoke. Although they hadn't had a drink, in their minds they toasted their luck in coming out alive.

OLD MONTREAL

AS THEY MEANDERED THEIR way through the narrow streets, taking care not to catch their heels in the cobblestones, they chattered excitedly about the guys they had just met.

They couldn't believe it. They were still freaking out! They had just met the nicest guys ever! How could that one guy be a convicted felon? He was so cute, so nice, and so genuine.

His name was Justin. He was here with his two friends from small-town Vermont to catch the Lil Wayne Show last night. Tonight they were doing the tourist thing down in Old Montreal. He had to be lying. OMG.

The conversation only came up because one of them asked why the boys didn't drive up from Vermont. Why did they have to hitchhike? Then, as if they had opened a tap or something, all the rich and impressive details came flying out. It was almost like a badge of honour. The girls found themselves intrigued and attracted to this guy. He was so lovable, so…helpless. They could have eaten him up even in hearing his story.

Charged on fifty-eight counts of burglary, convicted of eighteen of those charges. Twenty years old, father of a three-year-old girl the mother wouldn't let him see. Trying now to complete high school…collective sigh, ladies. Out of jail early for good behaviour and participating in a substance abuse program and personal therapy. Carrying a letter of permission to leave the state from his parole officer…but he was just so nice!

Too bad they couldn't hang out. Too bad they had to catch their ride back tonight. (That's okay, because they exchanged email addresses). ;)

ANGELS AND CRICKET

THERE ARE ALWAYS THOSE who choose not to go the traditional route for any number of reasons and for any number of occasions. They are often rebels, with or without a cause. Or they just can't buy into the hype surrounding prom night. Or they don't have the necessary funds to buy in. Or they truly want just to make it their own.

For whatever reason, this group exists and has a different type of fun, a different point of view, and a different, albeit not less memorable, prom night.

When writing these stories I found myself naturally gravitating toward the groups that didn't follow the crowd. I want to share one personal and poignant experience about what I have come to think of as two of My Prom Girls.

There is one magical moment that resonates in my mind. When I close my eyes, I can easily conjure up the beauty of that sultry night.

It was a perfect summer evening with limos, balloons, and banners that said, "Congrats, Grads!" The guys were hauling suit bags while running to catch the bus, and the girls were fresh from the spa. For another group of grads, there was another far less hurried experience happening in a mega store parking lot.

This event took place shortly after a few well-publicized stories involving the unfortunate misuse of the Sikh ceremonial kirpan. This incident had surfaced in the news, along with the continuous, long-winded debate over the right to wear traditional headgear and carry the kirpan.

With that recent news and the hoop-a-la surrounding it still fresh in my mind, I spotted what looked to be a gathering of some sort in a large empty parking lot. Being one who is naturally drawn by curiosity to crowds, I drove slowly to get a better look. My immediate sense was that there was going to be a rumble—a big time rumble. I spotted the white turbans and the unmistakable figures of adolescents as I heard a heated exchange in loud voices. They were definitely arguing about something. My hand instinctively grappled for my phone. I was about to save someone from getting stabbed with a kirpan! Or worse, maybe shot or beaten to a pulp! This peaceful summer night was about to explode right before my eyes, and I had no intention of letting any of these poor misguided kids hurt each other. Not on my watch. No sireeeee.

Imagine my surprise, delight, embarrassment, and flood of relief as I slowed down and drew closer to this happening. I drove so close that it became very clear what they were doing.

In that parking lot on that hot summer night, was a large group of well-dressed young men, wearing white turbans, and even white kurtas. They were innocent, beautiful, and somehow sacred against the starry night sky. And they were…just playing a simple game of cricket….

Had I just experienced cultural bias? What the heck! I felt ashamed of my initial reckless conclusion about these young men. However, my faith in my personal belief system washed my shame away, allowing me to experience fully the awe of the moment (a legitimate *Awe* moment). As I paused, I could almost envision the dance of Punjab and swear I detected the distinct sound of a sitar playing.

I didn't stay long or look hard. It suddenly felt like I was invading a private moment. Again, I remembered the many reasons why I love living in Montreal.

This treasured memory, which resonates as clearly today as it did that night, is the reason I sent My Prom Girls to the parking lot when they were out roaming aimlessly, talking, giggling, and dreaming prom night away—off the beaten path. Thanks guys. Your secret is safe with me.

TOO LATE FOR MISS MONTREAL

LOOKING ON ARE THE guys who seem to show up everywhere that tradition requires, taking in the sights, enjoying their own company, and organized in their own peculiar way. For some odd reason, the girls missed the Miss Montreal Boat. All their plans came crashing down around them as they sprinted to the already **departed boat**. What bad luck. No dinner, no classmates, no alternate plans.

They need not have worried. The whole ship had their plans crushed as it was. The boat returned within a half an hour as the ambulance pulled up and waited for the coroner to remove the body of a victim of his own demise. A seventeen-year-old heroin junkie had overdosed.

HOTEL CHECK IN

MAJOR CITIES ALL OVER the world have a strict and very exacting check-in and booking policy. Not Montreal.

A few major/minor incidents on prom night (but only in recent years), has prompted hoteliers to require not just a credit card, but the holder of the credit card, if they live in the area, to come on site and register the room in person.

This provides only a petty inconvenience. Parents march dutifully downtown to take care of the task, warning their child within an inch of their lives that there are to be **NO** free-bees for anyone, no booze in the room, no extra kids even if they pay. The parents essentially entrust their charge to be in charge, or pay the price.

Parents won't agree? They forbid you from staying in a downtown hotel? *No problem.* Easy fix is in the wings. Credit cards are a dime a dozen. Blackmailing or calling in a favour from your own or someone else's older brother or sister quickly puts the stress of the hotel booking behind you. There is a decided disadvantage to this method as they will crack under parental pressure or rat you out fast if you screw them over. Thanks to the magic of prom night, even if one of your parents find out, they either (1) won't tell the other parent, or (2) already knew to begin with. Historically, you can pretty well get away with mayhem and bedlam on prom night. The puzzlement lies steeped in the tradition and that's what I'm talkin' 'bout.

Of course, all the rules, threats, and warnings become semantics come prom night when there are **NO RULES**. Threats are acceptable and expected, and the warnings bounce back to the one warning so fast you can almost see the deflection.

Montreal holds true to its reputation on those spring weekends where hotels are teeming with young "visitors"; where cases of alcohol are "snuck in"; where the patrons scurry past the front desk already with key in hand, provided by the credit card holder who checked-in on their behalf just after 11 a.m.

There is chaos in the city and things are just heating up. What's not to enjoy?

As soon as the girls have run to the washroom, made ride arrangements, and have said their last minute "see-you-theres," organized chaos ensues as the mad dash for the hotel room follows. These three are in fact tired already. Some will pluck down in the hotel room where others will use the facilities as an enormous changing room, stopping just long enough to catch their breath before heading out to the clubs or other planned escapades.

Their load of accessories was best kept all together with thanks to one of their brother's old hockey bags. It beat the hell out of carrying all the stuff separately. They giggled as the limo driver and concierge tried to manipulate their "luggage."

All dressed up and ready to Party! The Girls hurriedly rush downstairs to the Hotel Lobby for another requisite Group Shot before heading out once again into the eventful evening.

BALLER: THE "AFTER PROM"

OKAY, SO YOU NEED to know if Baller and Pink sealed the deal. The answer is yes, indeed they did. Two birds killed with one stone since Baller had not in fact done "it" before, but rather just let his friends fantasize as much as they wanted to. He just never denied it.

After a tumultuous few weeks leading up to prom night and the disaster at the hotel dinner because of that stupid stoned DJ; after losing his hat; after Pink's reaction to his special effort; after all that, it felt so good to finally be alone with her and just relax. This prom stuff was far too taxing on him. He was stressed to the max.

He did have experience and knew instinctively what girls liked. For instance, on Valentine's Day he gained some valuable experience. Baller found out the hard way that girls like to talk about feelings after making out. Wow! Do they ever just NOT want to talk? Baller didn't love her anyway, so he wasn't really crushed when she blew him off. He figured that he had learned something really handy to use on the next love of his life, which happened to be lying beside him right this moment.

All of a sudden, Baller felt the need to practice his pillow talk. He was totally and completely floored. He jammed down hard against her reaction to the feelings he had just shared with her.

What? All he said was that he was really pissed at how she reacted to the bow tie corsage and how much her reaction had bummed him out, and how that had almost ruined the night for him.

What? Pissed is a legitimate feeling. It means angry! So why the hell SHE got so pissed at him and threw him out in such a hissy fit way was waaayyyyyyy beyond his scope.

His friends had warned him and warned him and warned him, and he just wouldn't listen, and now look! She was like one ugly screaming hyena. That must be what they were talking about. She must be PMSing big time. Holy shit! She was brutal. Thank you God that he was not a woman—Wow—Wow—Wow. Is it possible that just by asking her if she was getting her period soon, she would explode into *more* verbiage? Geezzzzuzzzz! She was not a very pretty picture right at this moment. What was all that black stuff on her face? She looked like a circus freak. Wow.

Baller picked up whatever he could grab and made a dramatic self-exit before he lost his temper for real. If she threw one more thing at him, he wouldn't be responsible for his actions. He had feelings too, ya know. Whatever! No, no! *Not* whatever.

He *felt* (See? That *feelings* word again—he had them too!) That he had put so much effort into that gesture and all she could yell about was the stupid Hummer her daddy rented, and the piece of crap corsage she gave him, and how she had paid for the hotel room and prom tickets…and on and on and on. Man! His boys were straight right: Girls just wanted rich guys to buy them stuff. It's really *the girls* who don't understand feelings. He was going to pay her back for the prom ticket, but he just hadn't gotten the chance yet. It was going to be a surprise, and now she could eat the ticket for all he cared. The dinner wasn't even worth it. It was a piece crap, just like this whole night.

Needless to say, Baller ended up in solitude on prom night. He walked around alone, wondering why none of his best buddies would answer their phones. He knows now that they were jealous, just like he thought. He feels it in his gut (though he fails to see why any of them would want to experience his babe's hissy fit). Speaking of gut, he felt like he hadn't eaten in a week. His stomach was killing him with hunger, or maybe it was still the malochio from all the jealousy going around. It could have been the crap dinner. It may have been that he scoffed all the party food…lol. They had *no idea*…Lol. Still, he wished he could call his mom to take it off, but he didn't want her to be worried and praying all night for him. He hated worrying his mom.

Rather than beating himself up further on the matter, he placated himself by picturing her being all alone in that great big Hummer that she never stopped gushing about. Serves her right, the bitch.

Baller allowed his thoughts to wander. She was a real "daddy's girl." She acted like some sort of princess. That would make her mother a queen, right? Her mother was a MILF. That's what she was, but he knew better than to tell her that. His friends were full of it. They all talked about her mother and how they were cougar hunting. It was all BS. They wouldn't have the cajones. Besides, kittens were so much more lively, playful, and cute.

Then he stopped thinking and headed for the mountain. The sun was coming up soon, and maybe he could hook up with his boys there.

In the meantime, he busied himself with a little rap mantra he had just made up, live to suit the occasion. Yes, he was a man of everything!

Dat u diss me.dnt piss me.get me all wrkd up.Look me live in d eye.I jist say wassup?

With all the right moves and all the right attitude, Baller managed to get past the incident that *almost* ruined *his* night.

He gave one last thought to his "prom princess" and felt (just for a moment) a little sorry that it turned out so bad, and that her night ended so early. With the vision of his weeping, lonely, heartbroken girl, he switched mind reels and went to blank for a while.

As Baller was switching reels, Pink was switching out of her tantrum mood and into her dancing shoes. Getting her act together at record-breaking speed she decided that absolutely nothing was going to stop her from enjoying the night she had planned out so caringly. Nothing at all. She took her time getting fixed, then ran to the lobby just in time for the group shot before heading out clubbing with her classmates and their friends.

IN Da CLUB

WAT? No ID? Doesn't matter here in Montreal, which is the long time host to partiers from every corner of the world.

The monstrous bouncer, who appears even bigger in life to the throngs of students looking to make their way into the club. He appeared to be smiling in a knowing way as if he had seen this scene and knew all the tricks possible. Rather than dole out grief to the partiers he made their night even more exciting with his slyly asked questions and careful winks. He loved his job and all it entailed. Tips included.

For generations Montreal has produced some of the finest party ambience, even producing the less-than-prestigious title to the World Class McGill University of "Best Party School". Much to the chagrin of some inhabitants and McGill Board members this dubious title cannot be denied.

At one time, the term VIP really meant VIP, but it has become a common name for "private party," which, today is not all private after all. Young promoters working for the club(s) do a great job making sure the VIP rooms are filled to capacity.

Montreal clubs are renowned for hosting the best parties within a 1,000-kilometer radius. It's part of what makes Montreal tick. It provides a playground for the rich and famous as well as a training ground for the fourteen-year-old rookies. It is a milieu that represents the liberal majority, and we take pride in knowing that we can out-rock any other Canadian city. Even the oldest inhabitant enjoys reminiscing about "back in the day" when it comes to Montreal nightlife.

Prom goers have to contend with the great big bouncer. But the right outfit, right look, right tip, right club, or right timing will get you in with *no ID* required. All it takes is the will power to make it happen. One club turns you away? No problem. Go next door. Simple fix to a non-problem.

For those who haven't gone to a club, prom night provides the perfect opening to check it out. Either the parents will pretend not to know where their prom goer is headed, or they will whole-heartedly support it because they did it too.

We've got something for everyone: VIP packages, party buses, high school, CEGEP, university promoters, and prom night specials. Everyone knows someone who can make this happen.

The girls, dressed in their ultra-club dance wear were getting their groove going. The raised platform held them somewhat precariously as "les boys" took in the sights with exquisite enjoyment. It seemed to be a better show than usual on prom night. The skirts were shorter, the dancing more provocative, and the mood so much higher than their regular weekend jaunts.

Once again, this remains a major part of traditional prom night in Montreal, preceded very briefly by the Hotel check-in. It is no wonder that the hotel room, originally booked with two to four guests, subsequently becomes a barrack with twenty overnighters.

SOLO

STILL UNABLE TO FIND HIS friends or get some food, Baller resigned himself to the fact that the night was over. Nothing exciting was going to happen and it could not get worse than this. He couldn't have been more wrong.

He finally found a secluded spot to sit down. Baller was exhausted with all that had taken place so far. His stomach was really killing him now. As he crouched to sit on the rock, Pink's phone (which unknown to him was in his back pocket) hit the speed dial to the local radio station where the Director of Marketing was taking the phone shift for the night, while troubleshooting how to boost the ratings for the sweeps. He couldn't afford to drop the ball on this and didn't mind putting in some extra hours. At the very moment he picked up the phone, Baller felt a big relief in his stomach as he broke wind time and time again. What the hell did he eat? *Who cares?* he thought, as he forced a more exaggerated noise into the night.

The barrage of gas emissions continued. He jumped up, and started shadow boxing and screaming at the top of his lungs, "I'm Baller Unpronounceable-Last-Name, and I'm King of the Freakin' Prom," followed by the unmistakable Rocky theme daaa da da da. Right out of his over-exaggerated big mouth and directly onto the digital tape at the radio station.

They had just implemented the "butt phone" policy. Although they had caught a few good ones, nothing compared to Baller's performance and nothing ever would. It just got better and better.

The Director of Marketing was swimming in his own creative juices, thanking God for his mercy, and, in between fits of laughter, patting himself on the back for ingenuity. He dropped to the floor in prayer, crying with relief and laughter. He had been under tremendous pressure this year and was functioning in an unhealthy state until tonight.

It had been a slow night because of prom, but in return, the prom had given him a gift. It gave him all the time in the world to plant this stuff. In his rush to start publicizing this bonanza, he had left the tape on.

He was busy alerting all of his personal friends on Facebook (1,456 and counting), all of the station's fans (who-knows-how-many and counting), all the Twitter subscribers. His marketing list was going full throttle and at lightning speed as he signed into MSN to let some more people into the loop. He'd keep them guessing. This was radio magic, and he was handling the controls. The "prank call campaign" combined with the "butt callers" should about round it out for him. God, he loved technology!

Oblivious to his surroundings and still basking in the moonlight, his earphones now blasting while he hooted and hollered the night away, Baller never heard the cop car pull up.

In the meantime, back at the radio station the marketing guy had tuned in once again to the phone call, and once again took delight in his ingenuity.

The police were having a slow night. With way too many patrols on duty tonight, they were pretty well just cruising, drinking coffee, and shooting the breeze. Pure boredom had brought them over to Baller. It was pure bad luck for Baller because he had just lit up his last spliff to celebrate feeling okay for the first time tonight.

He stopped mid-pirouette when he caught a glimpse of the police car, swallowed the joint (too late), and chocked up their visit to racial profiling. Though it hadn't happened to him in a while, he heard about it all the time: The cops just randomly picking on someone. He wasn't worried *at all.* He was clean—super-clean—hands down. By the time they got out of the patrol car, he was ready with attitude and felt skilled to take them on.

Once again he was mistaken. And once again, the night turned sour right before his eyes. What Baller had not realized, or even given any thought to, was that he had an unpaid speeding ticket still outstanding from a year and a half ago. At the time (and to this day btw) he didn't think he should have to pay the ticket because his probationary points had been wiped out, and he lost his license anyway. Life really sucked man. It really sucked. Nothing made any sense. Who would pay a ticket when they are no longer allowed to drive? All his friends agreed: Don't cough up the funds for nothing.

One minute he was actually having a good time (under the circumstances), and the next minute he was in cuffs and being processed at the Station. He felt like he was getting punked.

For the twenty-five millionth time in his short life Baller wondered when he would catch a break. When was it going to be his turn to live large? How the hell would he get through this one? Why was he in a jam tonight of all nights?

Meanwhile back at the station, the marketing director still had uncontrollable laughter, tears of joy rushing out of his eyes, and a stomachache of his own from the hilarity he was feeling. He was picturing living large himself. Finally.

MINOR :~(INCONVENIENCE)

No matter how well planned the night is there are enviably a few more wrinkles than anticipated. That older limo that the girls nabbed at the last minute ended up breaking down. The rain ensued indicating spring had in fact arrived. Luckily, Montreal has a great underground transportation system that carries the girls safely from place to place. The underground city helped save dresses, hair, shoes and tempers from bringing down the night.

AS THE CLOCK STRIKES THREE

ON ANY SATURDAY OR SUNDAY morning, as Montrealers head for the mountain, it is impossible to miss the line up that is certain to have formed at Beauty's at the base of Mt. Royal. Tradition, therefore, is called on once again as the night is heading toward dawn. Beauty's tables are filled with hungry teenagers chatting. Although exhausted, they are not about to miss the chance to watch the sunrise over Mt. Royal with those with whom their bonds lie: Their fellow prom goers, who have almost managed to make it 'til dawn.

As my three guys (who should not go unnoticed, having stuck with their plan all the way) can attest, the night has been a full one. The girls all look the same by now. Their blend of beauty—hair, dresses, charm, and splendor—is having only a limited effect, if only because of the sheer numbers of them visible through the murkiness. The novelty and excitement have wound down, the dramas have all unfolded, and they just want to sit down and have a bagel. They are on the home stretch. No hits, no runs (save one), and no errors. It's been a good night. They are silently content with their decision after all to do their own thing. They hung with tradition, too, in their own sweet way.

Now they just wanted to feed their growling stomachs and ease their tired feet but not a seat was to be found as others mulled around restlessly, waiting for the same.

THE BAIL OUT

THERE WAS NO GD way he was staying in lock-up. It was brutal. If he could, he would have burned his tux on the spot, but they confiscated his Zippo. If he didn't find someone soon to bail his ass, he would be burned when he hit the cell in this get-up. He was *not* spending Prom night in a cell with losers, drunks, and junkies.

Inwardly frantic at this point, he tried again desperately to reach his "friends." Still no answer. Screw them for life! He just didn't have it in him to call his parents; he just couldn't do that to them. They would die. His GF was out of the question, and besides, her line was always busy! WTF!

Bail plus the ticket was a hefty amount. He had $17.58 in his account. Just wouldn't cut it.

Baller forced himself to concentrate. Who did he know with money? Like a thunderbolt, it struck him. By that time he couldn't even think anymore, his anxiety was through the roof, and that's how he ended up calling Pink's home number and begging her father to come and help him out. Baller forced himself to remain calm, but it was all he could do to hold back the tears of relief when her dad agreed to come downtown and assured him it was going to be okay.

Ecstasy hit the radio station guy as he saw the gift before him. Fifteen minutes of fame (after the edit and with a spread of segments strung over the next seven days like a soap opera). It was too good to be true. Too good. He was disappointed when Baller found the phone in his back pocket, and the line finally disconnected. The manager continued to work on his campaign well into the next day, driven by the sheer force of good fortune, and the hope of some kudos for himself for a change.

You may wonder what on earth possessed Pink's dad to agree to bail his daughter's ditched prom date out of jail (yes, she called and told them half the story) at this ridiculous hour. It was a very simple two-part explanation: First, relief that his daughter had ditched the guy, and second, dad himself had been there, done that, and burned the T-shirt years ago.

For Dad, it was the night of his twenty-eighth birthday. He was living in lower Westmount (it was cheap back then), fresh out of law school, loans up the wazoo, making peanuts at his articling job when he, too, was arrested. As an educated young advocate, he had helped lead the neighbourhood coalition that was formed to fight overnight parking tickets that beseeched the neighbourhood. None of his neighbours, who were recipients of these tickets, paid them. They were determined to put forth a united front in a fight with city hall. They believed that the power of their numbers would prevail. The fight had gone on long enough for a substantial amount of unpaid tickets to be noticed. Although the fight had begun, the battle was not over, and neither side showed signs of budging.

He was hurrying to meet a large group of his friends to celebrate. As he raced down St. Catharine and crossed at the corner of Guy he neglected (ha) to stop running, even though the light was red. In Toronto, they call it j-walking. Here it is called, "Keep it moving, people." Meanwhile, a car some cowboy was driving managed to hit him as he darted across the street. Unhurt but a little shaken, he took the hand offered when he tried to get up. He thanked the police officer and went to hurry back on his way, assuring the officer he was fine. The officer, obliged by law, retained him, made sure of his well-being, sent off the driver once he had checked him out, and processed Pink's dad's ID.

Here's the scenario:

- He was j-walking; there is a fine. (Surprised?)

- The car that hit him was not at fault.

- He had fifty-two outstanding parking tickets.

- There were no cell phones back then.

- *All* of his friends, his brother, and his sister, were waiting at a street corner for him.

- He was a GD lawyer who got himself arrested. He was totally humiliated and pissed.

As he waited for Baller to emerge, and after taking care of the fines and bail, Pink's dad knew he could clear the kid. He made an out-of-character snap decision to hire Baller as a runner at his firm for the summer. He would boost the salary a bit so he could be "paid back" for the bailout, court appearance, and fines by just taking it off the top of Baller's pay cheque.

Thanks to the bridges and highways being in a perpetual state of construction, they had lots of time to shoot the breeze while they eventually managed the detours in spite of someone having changed all the signs. It allowed time for Pink's dad to realize that life had passed him by far too quickly and he, oddly, hadn't really felt this alive in years. He found himself, in a way, envying Baller's place in existence. One thing was for sure. Life was not going to pass him by any more.

 Baller had a feeling his luck was about to change for good. He was determined not to let life pass him by anymore, also. He was going to grab that brass ring. Yes, the old Baller luck was In Da House! A summer job at a prestigious law firm and a chance to throw it out at both his friends and Pink! Yes. Yes. Yes. This was it! He was certain. Dead certain. Everything seemed good at this moment, but only because he was totally oblivious to a couple of things: The "Butt Campaign," and the fact that his math teacher (head of the math department) had just accepted a position to head up the Pathways to Math department at the local collage Baller would be attending.

MT. ROYAL AT SUNRISE

AS IT ALWAYS HAS, and hopefully always will, the sun comes up over Mt. Royal every morning. But nothing can compare with sunrise following prom night, as the patrons of the night gather in solidarity and surprising silence to watch what Montrealers have enjoyed for decades. The sun coming up over the city they cherish.

The guys are just a few steps behind as the **Prom Girls** make their climb just in time to see the sun indicate a brand new day.

Long live traditions!

ONE LAST COFFEE

NOT WANTING THE NIGHT to end, the girls head to a café for one final conversation before heading home. They are satisfied, spent, chock full of memories, and anxious to start the summer now. Of course, not without catching a few hours of sleep before heading out to a relatively new addition to Tradition: "The Day after Prom Brunch."

One or two more photo ops present themselves before the prom girls call it a night.

The girls pause again and again, delaying the final goodbyes of the evening before starting to prepare for the brunch scheduled four hours from now.

Some still have the energy and choose to continue dancing.

HEADING

HOME

And still anything
goes…anything at all.

When or if they finally do sleep,
some completely miss the brunch,
and dream the day away in a sound
slumber.

Which ends up being no big deal.

Because
it is
summer
after all,
and
everyone
knows
that
anything
goes, right?

Eventually, as they pile out of the limo, each with their own private thoughts and quiet good-byes, they can't help but think, "Gee, I wonder what a limo will go for when it's our tenth year high school reunion?"

Bye for now Girls ! It's been Marvelous!

There should be no
surprise that this book
is dedicated to Prom
Girls everywhere.
Prom Girls past,
present, and future.
I salute you and
thank you
profoundly
for your
contributions
to me.

In particular, to a very
special one, closest
to my own heart,
I would like to say:

Good night Eva,
sweet dreams,
God bless,
you know the rest...
forever.

Love Mom

CHANGE THE WORLD

Only a few of thousands of small ways to help Change the World

JOIN THE THOUSANDS WHO volunteer each year to work with a fabulous, established organization, whose model is built on "giving a hand up rather than a hand out" to those in need. They work all over the world, giving the gift of decent living conditions. www.habitat.org, www.habitat.ca

By volunteering with this organization you are giving yourself the gift of widening your knowledge base, see the world, interacting with others, teaming for a cause and learning to accept the world and its troubles while finding out why, first hand.

The benefits received by volunteers far out-weigh the effort involved. This concept has been repeated over and over. People who do volunteer are embarrassed by high praise, not that they are not proud but because they carry this secret. The only way to feel the way those who benefit is to go ahead and commit.